Black Women With Tamales

Stories

by Lorraine Gow

Black Women with Tamales

This is a work of fiction. Names, characters, businesses, places, events and incidents are either the products of the author's imagination or used in a fictitious manner. Any resemblance to actual persons, living or dead, business establishments, locales or actual events is entirely coincidental.

ISBN: 978-1-6880303-4-3

Library of Congress Control Number: 2020900696

Cover and logo image by Diana Huang

Black Women with Tamales

The women in these short stories came to America seeking a reversal of the usual in their lives. Being black Spanish-speakers, they experienced life on a tightrope, balancing public expectations, family traditions, and their own desires. As immigrants, they faded into the background like worn wallpaper in a closet until removal, leaving its aged adhesive tarnished or admired by an unsuspecting newcomer.

for Estela Agatha Casanova
and Angela Estela Smith

"The people who give you their food
give you their heart."
Cesar Chavez

CONTENTS

FAULT LINES

"There is no such thing as a life of passion any more
than a continuous earthquake . . ."

Lord Byron

Earthquake fault lines are born from geological rifts that straddle California from Cape Mendocino to the Mexican border. When there is a violent slip along the fault lines, the movement can cause sudden, rough upheavals. These faults, however, are nothing compared to the emotional, ragged edges of the hopeless who live along those same fault lines, people ill-prepared for the noise and uncertainty of living in cities subject to tectonic shifts.

Just as with earthquakes, my family of marginalized immigrants never knew when we would have an eruption caused by financial upheaval or an apartment eviction. For us, the slippage rate along the fault dangled between *we'll pray harder* to *we'll take the next Chevy back home.* My family's possessions were uncomplicated: dark clothes, a Bible, one sacred sterling silver spoon and fork set, and the ghosts of past upheavals. Our ghosts did not merrily ride along with us like the jovial spirits at the end of the Haunted Mansion ride at Disneyland. No, our ghosts terrified us – causing us to step in shit, forcing us to make unwise decisions.

The burden of living in an earthquake zone with these ghosts was intensely more difficult. The ghosts reminded us that life was fleeting, but they never apologized. We were a family of black, Honduran immigrants cornered into an ambiguous role: we did not know from which direction disaster would strike or which fault would demand immediate penance. Penance was a cost always calculated into our meager monthly budget.

My mother and I were enigmas to the other people in the neighborhood we called home: black people who spoke Spanish, made tortillas and red beans like Mexicans, and didn't attend the local AME Church on Sundays. However, as with many families on our block, our men – the fathers, the grandfathers – were absent, but the "uncles" were abundant, too many to count, too many to wish upon a star, too many to feel safe. My father and grandfather resided within our closet of ghosts, still not providing the love and nourishment that we needed, still not shielding my mother from the earthquakes.

Living in the Golden State requires a constant vigil, for the earthquakes rumble without prior warning. At 7:00 a.m., a tremor began. Our house teetered, cracks began to appear in the plaster walls, and dishes slid out of their cabinets and crashed on the kitchen floor. But most alarming of all was our rising fear. Six seconds into the seventh hour of the new day, the earth stopped shaking. Coffee had spilled onto the floor where my mother sat in a puddle of urine, determined not to move until things were still. "Mario, Mario, Mario!"

"There is no Uncle Mario here today. No Mario, Mamá," I explained. Uncle is what I call Mario. Mamá has never spoken of him. I assume he is my father or her lover.

The mixture of liquids on the floor filled the kitchen with a scent that signaled the fault lines had been disturbed.

"Damn, that was quite a shake so early in the morning," my mother began as she continued to sit in a widening pool of colored water, "get the mop now!"

Mopping up foolish messes was a chore I learned before I could read. On any given day, even when the sky signaled that running with white butterflies was a natural pastime for a playful girl, a mop was placed in my small hands, and the order was given to wipe up the unpleasantries created by my mother. I never managed to navigate corners without leaving some of the mess in the ninety degree angle, so my mopping was referred to as "half-assed."

Like an underpaid church janitor, I rolled out the yellow bucket with the attached mop and began the job of keeping my mother sane. Soon I could say with pleasure, "All done."

"These quakes unnerve me!" my mother ranted as she moved from the floor to the bathroom, where she began to shower off the morning's misery. And before the shower water turned tepid on her back, she yelled to me, "Bet you didn't get the corners!"

* * * *

The slippage of our family's fault lines took place about once a month when something triggered a memory, or when rent was past due, or when our nomadic lives became stuck in wet sand. But the story of my father was the cause of the most slippage.

"¡*Mija, mija!*" My mother cannot call me by my name. She had obfuscated the event of my birth by saying my father's last name was Vasquez, and that's about all she had ever cared to share about him.

"¡*Mija, el terremoto*! ¡*Mija, el terremoto!*"

"Come have breakfast. There will be no more earthquakes today. Did you have a nice shower?"

"The water was too cold, and then it was too hot. I think the ghosts wanted me to suffer right then and there. I'm an old woman, and they are still angry with me. Am I to enjoy no goddamn peace?"

"It is not the way of our family to have peace, so please do not bother the ghosts with your funny thoughts, Mamá."

14

"What is funny about these thoughts is that you think I don't remember you and the day you came back into my life after being born dead. You know, you are a ghost yourself!"

"Mamá, why have you always said that I came back from the dead?"

"I want more coffee. More coffee!"

Pouring the hot coffee into my mother's mug brought a smile to her face. She took several sips and ate two fork servings of the scrambled eggs I had made. Then she called me *Maria*.

"Maria? My name is not Maria. Who is Maria?" When the foolish question left my mouth, I remembered the trouble curiosity caused the cat. Maybe I *was* already dead.

"You are. That was the name I gave you when *la Madre* took you away. She was what Americans call a midwife. To pregnant women back home, she was just the fat woman with big hands and big breasts who knew the spells of the old Africans."

This was new lore my mother was creating on the spot.

"Tell about *la Madre,*" I prompted.

"Who? Oh, la Madre. . ." My mother drank more coffee, then motioned with her chin that she wanted toast.

"*Ah sí, la Madre* was a black Carib from the Mosquito Coast, another nomad seeking shelter and finding none until she helped deliver a child with potential, and the child's father had shown extreme gratitude. Don Miguel had set up *la Madre* as his wife's wet

15

nurse and his back porch mistress. You know how those south-of-the-border stories go. *El* patron died, the child lived, and the widow and *la Madre* became intertwined into a close friendship."

"The toast is delicious. Sourdough bread?"

"Ah huh. Well, did *la Madre* deliver me?"

"The earth was not silent on the night you were born. It coiled tightly around itself, then began to sway. And there I was, frightened and hurt by the man I was forced to live with. He had done this to me, and I spat out his name over and over and over – Gustavo Jaime Maria Vasquez."

The lore and tenderness ended as quickly as they had begun. My mother lapsed into silence, slowly chewing the sourdough toast, searching the small kitchen for wall cracks her thoughts could escape into without notice, without disrupting the stillness.

"*La Madre* poured dark rum down my throat, and I pushed and pushed . . . I heard nothing. *La Madre's* face told me those months of confinement were wasted. !*Basta*!"

"*Basta*? No! No, no, no! We're not d—"

"But you see, we were done. You were dead. *La Madre* rested your limp body on my swollen belly, and her tears and my tears did not bring life to you. Gustavo Jaime Mario Vasquez cursed your body and left us alone with *la Madre*. The black Carib woman wrapped you in a torn gypsy dance skirt. It had red ric-rac on the border and was made from rough cotton. She placed you in the corner of the room

16

where I lived. It wasn't two minutes after *la Madre* placed you there that the earth began to shake as if the devil himself was angry with our village. The rafters of the house howled like scared animals. *La Madre* ran out and told me to follow, but I could not leave you. If *el Señor* wanted it, I would be as dead as you. I curled myself next to you, removed the gypsy skirt, and held you to my chest. You and I were abandoned as the ground shook and walls fell, and people begged God's forgiveness. The *terremoto* stopped and your mouth opened. Opened. My fear and your determination held back those old walls. I had wanted to call you Maria to honor your father, but he left us. I named you *Yesenia* because of the gypsy skirt you had been wrapped in. And as you have grown, I have hoped you would become as unencumbered as that red ric-rac. That was always my secret wish for you. Instead, you have been encumbered with me."

Once again, the kitchen was still; all the words that were to be spoken had been spoken. My mother finished her breakfast and moved into the garden, where she would rewrite the scriptures. This was the only time she had spoken of my birth, and I am not sure if this new lore was the fantasy of a woman overcome by a lifetime of being on the run or the absolute truth. After all, we are nomads, and nomads do not deal with absolute truth. Our truth lies in the fault lines that traverse our hearts. We forgo permanent fixtures, escaping what has been left behind and never turning around to look back.

17

BLACK WOMEN WITH TAMALES

"She has the oddest sense of being self
invisible, unseen; unknown . . ."

Virginia Woolf (*Mrs. Dalloway*)

The way into Tinamou Bay is the same way you leave – by sea. A notch on Nicaragua's Caribbean side, the coastal town, bordered by a nature reserve, is in many ways uneasy with its own quirkiness: cargo ships move by in silence; panga drug boat runners believe the town is cursed and prefer the corruption of Cuco, a much larger town further south; and the trade winds only gust when sea turtles mate. Tinamou Bay's most significant oddity, however, is its tamales made early on Wednesday mornings and said to be the source for bay people not seen or understood.

The dark faces of the Tinamou Bay people tell of an ancient mixture of African, Spanish, and Maya. It is said the Africans, who refused to be enslaved by white greed, were the ones who brought the ability to be seen and not seen to the bay people. Those who have visited the town all laugh at this claim just as hardily as the bay people themselves. A group of old women know different. The bay people call them shamans, and their journeys are spiritual but bothersome. I called one of those old women "Grandmother." My grandmother passed the gift of being obscure, hidden in plain sight, to me, but she forgot to tell me how to know if I was being seen or unseen.

The ability to stand outside my body came easily; I was born on the Moskito Coast and learned to make tamales quickly. I began my journey at the heels of my grandmother's feet by stirring the hot corn masa. Once I learned the proper texture of the masa, I was taught how to add the achiotê, sea salt, ground pink peppercorns, and hand-crushed tomatoes. Most importantly, I was taught to whisper the sound echoed by sea turtles as they lay their eggs. Although I never heard the sound myself, the echo was in my mind. That was all that was needed to be invisible. The night before the third Wednesday of September, my grandmother told me I needed luck, not lessons.

My mother and I left Tinamou Bay that Wednesday afternoon. We were leaving with a man who came to dive for gold doubloons. My grandfather called him a fool. Everyone in Tinamou Bay knew the treasures men sought were buried further down south by the cays and outer islands. My grandmother called my mother a fool. Every woman of Tinamou Bay knew to have a prayer answered quickly was usually a sign the prayer had been answered by Satan. On that day, I held my head up so high my tears could not roll down my face. I walked backwards into the sea – invisible to my mother and the diver, not wanting to forget my grandmother's face, not wanting to forget the recipe for the tamales.

Invisible women were not appreciated in America. We were just *Negroes* who spoke Spanish, cooked rice and red beans in coconut milk, and prayed to a white god called Cristo in a storefront and in the small apartment where we lived. The diver's family welcomed us with a sigh of betrayal dripping from their mouths. "Those people are all the same, no matter what part of the world they crawled from," they said.

During our first years in California, the tamales were made on Saturday mornings and sold after the 9:00 a.m. Mass on Sundays.

For years thereafter, as my mother became employed as a housekeeper for a family living in the Hollywood Hills, the tamales were made only for Christmas and, finally, only on the diver's birthday. We forgot the comfort and the talk of back home and became invisible – American style: no one noticed us and no one wanted to know us. It was during this regimented assimilation that the diver took a plane to Tortola and left my mother and me a letter of regret. Mother's heart ceased to pitter-pat. The local newspaper reported: *Immigrant takes life by walking into riptide.* The reporters didn't know my mother was trying to get back home.

"I was so shocked to hear about –" my mother's employer wept. She was silent for twelve seconds, a designer hanky adjusting her runny mascara. "You, you have my deepest sympathy." That done, the woman calculated the reality of needing someone to clean the house, cook the broccoli, take the children to gym, and walk the three dogs. "Oh, ah, would you like to have her position?" the employer asked.

"I still have two years of high school left," I said.

"You can finish high school at night and earn your diploma on your own time," she explained dismissively.

The forward progress the good old U.S. offered, which my mother and I had once spoken of with great glee, became a motif adrift. Reality righted itself within me, up my spine. When I thought about my position in the economic scheme of things, the only answer became evident. I was here to clean up the spills in my employer's life. I said "Yes." My life would now be lived off to the side as *her girl.*

Cousin Maria wrote a letter about her marriage to Luis Raul Mendoza. I did not write back to tell my cousin Maria about my picture in the local newspaper or about the day I was no longer invisible to people with money. I did not want to tell her how the riptide had once again returned to the city's beaches, and how I had saved the life of a boy, a young boy with blond hair and a gap in his teeth. "I didn't know black people could swim!" the boy explained to the reporters, and his father added, "My wife thought she just played in the sand while at the beach!" Some people called me brave, others said I was a *positive image.* No one asked if I wanted the fame: the keys to the city and my picture taken with the mayor, or the gratuitous check the boy's father gave me in front of onlookers. His wife later said he had acted in haste.

The public saw it differently. "Finish your education!" they shouted. "You now have enough for college!" Celebrityhood also changed the course of my employment. I no longer was *her girl,* but the savior of her son – an immigrant worthy of a cause, a cause my employer said she would orchestrate. My employer also wanted me to understand this new phase of my life would not interfere with my daily chores. "I have relatives coming this weekend, you know. Please refresh the guest rooms."

As with all jobs, there are days when rain falls even at night. That's when the sea turtles on Tinamou Bay bury their eggs when human eyes are closed, and those eyes still open belong to ghosts and the invisible ones. Maybe next Wednesday I will make tamales to feed my stomach. Or perhaps my invisibility will have to wait for my cause to vanish.

A SCHERZO FOR ANXIETY

". . . do not lose heart. Though outwardly we are wasting away,
yet inwardly we are being renewed day by day."

2 Corinthians 4:16-17

A corner provides ample square footage for a resuscitation from madness. Savannah Tucker reviewed the prerequisites for the slippage: hallucinations; a manageable size knife, six inches maybe; skipped medications; and voiced hesitations to herself. Choices, choices, choices. The corner, decorated with a white wooden chair and a maiden hair fern, accepted the challenge; there were no windows and peacefulness draped from the walls. The air in this part of the house carried hope.

However, the thought of suicide had escaped through the ceiling vents and floor registers. Savannah remembered being revived like some hooue-bound cat or a dysfunctional teenager in need of intervention – church-style intervention: *Yes, praise Jesus, she believes!* Savannah looked about her bedroom and saw no parishioners dressed all in white, waiting to place their hands upon her forehead while asking Jesus for deliverance. And a family intervention was even more of a joke. What family did she claim – two pound mutts, an ex-husband who finally admitted the Lord was his savior (not the women whom he compulsively fucked) and her collection of Limoges porcelain boxes. In her overmedicated catatonia, life was ordinary – dull, unrepentant. She used to be a good Christian of sorts, now people back home would say, *done lost her mind over a mon.* Savannah knew *she* wasn't too crazy; she just understood her place in the scheme of things – no place.

The mail-ordered Limoges sat on a sofa table. They added the required touch of having achieved the American dream for her Westside townhouse. Savannah had planned to place trinkets from her bouts with sanity in them, but she had none – neither the trinkets nor the bouts of sanity. She was an immigrant from Belize living in Los Angeles. The cadence of breathing in a big city had corrupted her mind, wrestled it to the ground until the thought of spending a day in raw sewage was a more comfortable alternative. Smeared feces on a concrete headstone would make for an interesting epitaph she thought: *And here lies the problem with my life – it stunk!*

This wrong had to be amended, and the perceived restlessness which had come and gone and returned with it had convinced Savannah it was time to take charge of her depression and render a life safe to venture outside – to socialize, to have a soul again. She sat in the white wooden chair, removed a compact from a purse, opened it, and admired its reflection. *Don't worry, I know you want to be the highlight of my life; powder your nose and do something with your hair. Black women have a hard time adjusting to graying kinks. You need to leave this house.* Savannah snapped the compact shut! She called upon the darker sisters of Bald Mountain to chart her day's course. *What do you want to come tomorrow?*

Savannah was late in taking charge of her life; a life that had belonged to so many others: the nuns at school, the uncles her mother brought home, and the games her mother and she played after each uncle left. There were some days when the games ceased to be appropriate. *Oh, those days you were not yourself, Mama.* Savannah had been her mother's house girl – the one to get whipped, blamed for the late rent, and charged with murder. She never denied any of it; after all, it was her mother and she was her mother's only child.

Dr. Joseph Borrero had been encouraging, with suggestions for improvement and even aplomb about the unwinding trail of her mother's bothersome death. He was from Mexico and understood the finesse of death. His family cleaned and decorated the graves of their loved ones each autumn on *Día de los Muertos* (Day of the Dead), then ate candy skeletons to support the spiritual journeys of the dead. Although the doctor-patient conversations between Dr. Borrero and Savannah earned mixed reviews, she was confident one pill less a week would be manageable. After all, change was a lesson taught to her long before time began to run backwards. She couldn't remember if she had told Dr. Borrero about the reverse progression of time. *Oh, catching up with time was a ruse used by fortune tellers on the unsuspecting masses* is what she should have explained to the doctor, not the sad story of her own reversal of life.

Savannah remembered the second hand of Uncle Gilbert's watch and their lessons together in a land where trees curtseyed when a princess entered the room, teddy bears caught tears in cupped paws, tea was served hot with honey – not sugar – and panties were hidden in the laundry basket afterwards. Savannah was an excellent student. The lessons were structured like a Chopin polonaise – a dance in triple time: fairy tales, insertion, redemption, repeat. Sometimes the repetition was justified, but on one occasion it was misread – badly misread. That's the time she had never forgotten, but she was always willing to try. *It wasn't love, was it?* That's what she should have told the doctor: *it wasn't love.* Instead, she recalled the whispers of the old adage recited by her grandmother, "*Nothing ventured, nothing gained.*" Savannah's grandmother kept secrets, like all women; she

28

manipulated a wrong into a right, or better yet, feigned ignorance. Savannah pleaded guilty by reason of insanity, but that was her secret. Dr. Borrero suggested a train ride. "Sit next to anonymous folks and participate in courteous social conversations about the weather, seasonal fruits or thoughts on shopping on State Street." She agreed, reassured that if anything out of sync occurred, she would conveniently blame it on Dr. Borrero; after all, it was his suggestion.

* * * *

The morning opened with two crab cakes and a cup of hot Darjeeling tea for breakfast. The plate was full, but something was missing. Fruit? Confusion? Her mother had ordered crab cakes when an uncle visited. Her mother had claimed its aphrodisiac qualities made men compliant. And again, Savannah had overthought her day and skipped her morning's dose. It was such a small, insignificant pill over which to fret after all; her life was cheap. She powdered her nose because that's what her mother would have done under the same circumstances. *Public display.* Her mother never appeared in public (at the bank or Sunday Mass) without a well painted face. *Who powders their noses these days*? That social grace belonged to her mother's generation, the generation that marched for total equality, then settled for far less. The millennials preferred tattoos and nose rings. Those accessories were not for the squeamish like herself.

29

Raspberry hair would be a much less punishing reflection of her pain – her surrender, her obvious decision to break with the pill regimen. This was such a compelling idea that she paid a local wig store good money for a raspberry human hair wig before sanity returned. Too much daylight for such high jinks. Savannah scolded herself for not returning the raspberry wig. Stepping out in the real world, it seemed, was not cheap. It was cumbersome. She clapped her hands, for the ubiquitous black mourning dress had become the perfect accoutrement to the raspberry hair wig. *Like Breakfast at Tif . . . no, better a donut from Suzy Liu's – one with purple, pink and white sprinkles.* Where would she hide the knife. People would say she was an old woman, probably suffering from a touch of early dementia, or an eccentric trying to recapture her youth. Her mother would have dismissed the black outer wear ensemble as a ridiculous attempt at punishing her own motherly efforts at proper wardrobe etiquette. Her mother had always taken Savannah's individuality as a slap to "mother's" wisdom. Today Savannah felt the presence of her mother more than usual. Once again, she excused these thoughts as the craziness returning.

A kitchen knife was too big, too expected; now a Swiss Army knife in black would do. *Mama is dead, and my evil thoughts buried her before the second anniversary of Uncle Gilbert's death.* A ride to the end of the line on Train 741 would be nice, as would the sullen memories of a male or two.

*   *   *   *

Ah, the coming spring would look better when whizzing pass urban's nature: over-stressed trees, rushed humans, and pit bulls blurred into an unrecognizable jungle of hues, a calming backdrop to end misery. Savannah feared no one or God's wrath. *Come, Spring, come!*

The train station sweated with humans scurrying themselves through the day before the weekend officially began. Commuters bumped into her, teenagers nodded agreeably at the raspberry hair, and older travelers, much older than herself, kissed loved ones goodbye – a return trip being a gamble. *Time. Ah, the morning rush.* Savannah almost returned to the safeness of her bed, her warm robe, the TV's remote, but a pair of hummingbirds tormenting each other forced her to take one step, then another. *What caused these small birds to be so pissed at each other? Certainly not the flowers, whose nectar they stole with relative ease or the atmosphere whose quietness they invaded with a thumping, numbing buzz. What pride their swift energy must afford them.* The more Savannah obsessed about the hummingbirds, the more she knew what she had to do on the train.

Before long, hallucinations careened into reality: Savannah was aboard the train in a seat, checking her pulse, searching the pit of her bag for the pill she forgot to take, nervously finding the compact knife instead. She nodded to strangers, signaling that she did not want a companion in the empty seat across from her. She had given herself the official alert – *Weirdo on board!* The raspberry wig just added to the entire ensemble. Being unsociable was tiring, and sleep came to Savannah with an unaccustomed haste. When her eyes did open, a young man sat where she had wanted no one to sit. An American hero – still in his Army uniform; still missing his left hand; still wearing his Uncle Sam's pride, a Purple Heart, on his left chest.

"Did you get that because of Afghanistan or Iraq or some drunken weekend miscalculation?" As the question left Savannah's mouth, she thought about its grit and demeaning grip. '*Why waste skepticism?*' she thought, "Well, which was it?"

"Afghanistan, ma'am." The young man tipped his head in deference to his female interrogator.

"I still don't know why we needed to be there long after our anger over 9/11 had been replaced by smart phones." Savannah removed her facial compact from her purse and dotted the shine from her nose. Then replaced it in her handbag.

"Ma'am?"

"Does it still hurt?" She leaned closer and gingerly stroked the stub which now functioned as a left hand. It was smooth, not showing any signs of trauma or the vicious political struggle which celebrated it.

"Every day, ma'am," His scraggly gaze drifted toward her. "Every day."

Savannah was silent, contemplating her next move without using an insult to hurl or cheeky quip to laugh about over a tall glass of beer. She stared into the young disabled soldier's eyes, grabbed his shirt collar, and pulled his lips to hers. Their embrace lasted several seconds longer than expected for an impromptu encounter. Once their lips unlocked, she opened her handbag, removed two Benjamins, and shoved them into the soldier's front pocket. "I truly do honor your sacrifice. I wish — " Savannah 's words were not important enough to be voiced. She sat back, her thoughts now roaming outside her body. The soldier was motionless, as her footsteps had been for the last month.

Savannah got up, moving cautiously through several cars of the moving train until she found two more vacant seats. She never once looked back at the Army Specialist. She dropped down into a vacant seat, exhausted, wondering when the hell she had taken to kissing strangers. She wiped off her lipstick and popped a breath mint into her mouth. Her mother never kissed strangers. Those men she brought home were not strangers, but old friends, uncles, long lost lovers trying to gain a foothold into her emotions. Mama never left the house without lipstick (nakedness belonged behind closed doors). Savannah removed the lipstick from her handbag, gave it a twist and traced the outline of her lips several times. When she returned the lipstick to her handbag, a man dressed to reflect his importance sat in the vacant seat. His smile was sociable, his gray hair combed so that tiny whiffs of it fell about his forehead just enough to hold one's attention, his messenger bag updated for impact.

"Do you mind?" he asked.

"Only if you don't mind that I surrender to your kindness," Savannah replied with a coquettish grin.

The businessman tried not to stare at the old woman with raspberry hair, but he was uncomfortable and could not control his mouth when he asked the obvious: "How did you come to that color?"

"I was inspired by the robes priests wear during Lent."

"Ah yes, religion. It can be such a crutch," he said.

"Only if you forget how to walk," Savannah replied. "I have never forgotten how to walk – except for that one time. And he was just an uncle, a friend of Mother."

The man with whom she shared the space lowered his head, smiled to himself, and cleared his throat as the train hesitated at the Glendale station. Of all the seats to pick – common urban nut case. "Yes, well, uh, ah, walking, I mean religion these days catapults us into disagreements, horrible wars," the man continued as he adjusted the headrest.

"You know, I never looked at religion that way. Two adversaries, each trotting out the splendor of their supreme beings, and each falling short," Savannah leaned closer to the stranger as she said those words, remembering Uncle Edmond and his rough hands, and the night those hands were almost severed by a kitchen knife.

"Each falling short! Yes, that is exactly what religion does. It falls six miles short of victory, and young men are supposed to bridge that gap!" The man dressed to reflect importance adjusted his suit, moving away from Savannah as much as possible in such cozy arrangements. The train slowed to a crawl as the conductor's voice overtook all conversations with an announcement that Train 741 had to pull over to allow a long freight train to pass.

"Blasted," the man said as he checked his watch.

"Uncle Edmond checked his watch the night he died. He was a post Korean War statistic on his way home from the VA Hospital. He unwisely stood in front of the Clematis Avenue Presbyterian Church when some white cop, determined to bring the mendacious ways of Mississippi to Los Angeles, shot him for being in a white neighborhood long after sunset." Savannah smiled as she whispered to herself, *Bless his ragged soul. I should have cut off his hand when I had the chance.*

"Pardon?" The man sitting across from Savannah said, astonished at her confession.

"Cut it off!" she shouted. Savannah did not know when she had begun to stand in a murderous pose with a train schedule in her right hand like a weapon, holding it over the stranger's head, her breathing heavy, her eyes glazed. "I, I, I am sorry," she apologized, slumping back down into the seat, checking the other passengers who were probably wondering about her mental fitness to be alone on a train. "It's all part of my delicate condition. That is what you say in public – *delicate condition*. Refined women usually did not display their rage in public." She excused herself, touching the handsome man's hands just a tad longer than strangers on a train should engage. "If you should see a black old woman with raspberry hair, remember she gave you the opportunity to share your views on religion." She then headed for the café car.

The freight cars were still taking their sweet time moving past Train 741, displaying corporate greed, America's dependence on oil, and our love for expensive European cars. *A drink was warranted; remembering the scars of one's life proved hazardous, especially on a train beginning to proceed.* The café car reigned four more cars toward the front of the train, a train reverberating from the age of the track spikes. The clickety-clack mantra pushed the rhythm of the day beyond what she had intended would be significant.

The legs of sixty-two-year-old Savannah Louise Tucker wobbled at the thought of walking half the length of the remaining train. She would make small human verbiages of *excuse me, pardon me, I'm O.K.* before booze placated the accident scene her morning had become. From the windows, she noticed the day had blossomed into a mixture of California sunshine and profundity; the San Fernando Valley remained witlessly dry, still wanting to be cool like L.A.

It was a perfect tourist day for realizing the golden sunshine

36

only gloss-coated the suddenness of death. She wasn't a tourist and her restlessness paused. *Had it been so bad a life? She had been abused to the point that nothing could have been done to make the pain less strenuous, to conceal her self-doubt about life or life's stumbling blocks. Maybe if she had been born blind or dyslexic, solutions might have been researched or annual telethons planned. There was nothing for a black girl raped by men who claimed to be uncles or at least interested in the folds of her mother's body. Had it been so bad a life? No children, one malfunctioned marriage, a mother whom she chaperoned into dementia, and the many drugs she took every night to forget. To forget all of it, but to remember the golden sunshine. She needed to lose weight; yeah, tomorrow she would have her last beef burger with cheese, bacon and chili peppers. Had it been so bad a life?*

The music was too subdued in the café car, or was it in her head? The train was moving faster now, faster past familiar scenes, old debts, and scoured locations, like a spent valentine. The train should have been on a mission to bring joy. Savannah decided she no longer needed to wait for *time.* A seat was available next to a window and across from a man probably dressed by his wife so that no other female would notice him, a domestic drinker. She ordered a double martini and told the bartender to hold the olive; she hated olives.

"The olives make it smooth," said the man in the seat across from Savannah.

"Did your wife give you that line to use?"

"Uh, oh, that's amazing! I thought I was being original," the man laughed. "My wife stopped promoting my humor years ago."

"At our ages, originality backpedals in an effort to make its arrival seem new."

"You're pretty quick on your feet for an old girl."

"Girl?"

"Isn't that what women over fifty call themselves? No offense intended, ma'am."

"None taken, old man. Girlhood is not a precious memory for me. I try to forget it whenever I can. Being black, poor, lonely, abused was no picnic; as a matter of fact, I went on my first picnic with mother and Uncle Raymond at the age of twelve. I haven't been on another since." Savannah tossed down the martini with earned relish. Train 741 glided on tracks too old to be so smooth, like a child's choo choo train heading for a mystical wonderland of cotton candy and endless hours of unsupervised play; instead this train rolled pass barrios proportioned off by gang logos spray-painted on anything, urban haute couture and the blandness of suburbia. Had it been so bad a life?

"Want another?" The man sitting across from Savannah asked. He waited patiently, looking pass the act of Uncle Raymond.

"One is my limit. Doctor's orders," Savannah graciously explained, although another martini would celebrate her choice to live another day.

38

"Yeah, I know what you mean. My heart is my complaint."

"It's still ticking; why do you complain?"

"That's about all it does. It can't skip a beat for love or practice somersaults out of fear. It has to remain calm, an unrealistic medical prescription for a seventy-year-old vet. I still crave a full throttle press into life's investments, but my heart has to take a second look when involved in pinprick conversations about life."

"Uncle Raymond was a vet. *'In this white man's army!'* Yep, that's how his deep voice classified his anger and his service to his country, but he liked picnics. You see, at a picnic freedom is everywhere: there are so many hiding places and rocks and trees to sneak behind, no commanding officers to call him *nigger*, and nature's monstrosities keep secrets and the tears of a young girl safe from sight." The older man who sat across from Savannah was still. He offered no compassion or outrage. He sat undisturbed by her recollections for several seconds, then said, "War is no toy." Both old train riders were silent, preferring to enjoy nature's scenery instead of conversation. Train 741 pulled, jerked, and hauled itself into a tunnel to the other side of Los Angeles, where a President's body lies, waiting for daily visits from conservative citizens and former campaign donors.

"This is my stop. You take care young lady," the man sitting across from Savannah said with a wink.

"I'm a gypsy – *one who forgot what it is to be free, to move*

39

without intentions – I just forgot the taste of fresh air."

As the man exited the train, Savannah shouted to him, "Is being a patriot a full-time journey?" The man stood on the platform motionless, just looking at Savannah as Train 741 rolled toward its next stop.

"Maybe I'll see you tomorrow," the old vet finally shouted back.

THE BANANA LEAF MIRACLE

"Grandmothers remember the days, the moments,
the miracles when the world was small and they,
themselves, were even smaller."

Y.L. Gow

Christmas Month, 1962
Los Angeles

It would be a Christmas of rice and beans and not much more. Our other pots would be stored in cabinets, still empty after being washed and dried. The family expected Mount Calvary, the local Baptist Church, to amend their holiday table with the addition of sweet potatoes in a pie and collard greens with pork fat – something this

Honduran family had never tasted. And gifts! A blonde-haired doll that talks and a dump truck with a workable payload. Our faithful Catholic foursome would worship the baby Jesus by singing *Las Mañanitas*, mourn our dead relatives and evaluate the passage to the 'States' as a sign that it was the right move even though the breadwinner now suffered from asthma, and the position at the county hospital had faded with her first gasp of California's dry, smoggy air. Abuela (Grandmother) held the family together by gathering prayers and damaged canned goods from the women of the Mount Calvary Baptist Church. The Catholic Refugee Center was twenty-seven miles and a bus transfer too far away for weekly visitation or the collection of alms. As with many newcomers to America, this family was a traveling minstrel show on hiatus – black faces speaking Spanish, saying the Rosary and eating tortillas all hours of the day. The women of Mount Calvary found the bunch of us curious . . . convertible. "Jesus Saves! Amen, Amen. Glory Alleluia!"

Our immigrant family embraced every opportunity offered in America, from a sparsely furnished, government-subsidized two-bedroom apartment in a housing project in South-Central Los Angeles to free Catholic education for two fatherless, baptized children willing to help clean the library after school to a sleep-in job opportunity Abuela secured with a white family in North Hollywood. Her aged bones cleaned three toilets, five bedrooms, pacified a colicky eight-month-old infant, and managed a kitchen where boiling water involved mastering an electric stove. Abuela's employers were determined to be "celebrities" even if it meant their housekeeper went home every other weekend and didn't understand the protocols of being a black person in "Hollywood" working for a white family in "Hollywood." When back home, the weeks before Christmas were spent making gifts and *nacatamales* and trying not to sin before Santa arrived.

I am ten years old, and my cousin, Nicholas, is nine. We are being raised as brother and sister, but we are not. We are joined by sisters: my mother married a man from Alabama with six children and a dead wife. Seven is an ill-fated number, so I was left with Nicholas' mother, a job she unwillingly accepted because Abuela reminded her that sisterhood is forever. Besides, my other aunts found U.S. husbands while Nicholas' mother was still unwed, like my mother, before she found her American hero.

"We need a miracle," I told Nicholas, "or our Christmas will be as cold as the concrete floor in this government project place."

"What can we do? We have no money and no prospects of open doors," Nicholas replied in Spanish.

Open doors was Abuela's acronym for *opportunity*. All our doors had been bolted shut. "I wish we could have *nacatamales* on Christmas Eve like we used to back home."

"*Si*, but everyone in L.A. eats Mexican tamales that are wrapped in corn husks."

"Maybe L.A. has no banana trees."

"I know where there are some banana trees. There are many big trees over by Watts. If we could get the leaves, then all we'll need is the *dinero* (money) for the ingredients."

"You are not supposed to be playing so far away from home. Bad people live over there. You say there are bananas trees there? True?"

"Ah huh."

"No, no, no, Jesus will watch over us." I crossed myself three times. "Your mother's asthma will end soon, and she will go back to work at the big hospital. We'll have money!" An optimistic appraisal of our situation ends the thought of searching for banana leaves. Anyway, what would we do for the rest of the nacatamales?

I am three inches taller than Nicholas, but as a male child, he explores places I could only imagine. Still, I could think of nothing else except making the nacatamales for Christmas Eve. When my aunt has asthma attacks, I do all the cooking, baking and making of traditional foods when Abuela is not home. Before the late autumn day ended, my soul was restless with plotting a walking trip into Watts. I paced around like some hungry animal, convincing myself that it would be a dangerous, but-not-too-dangerous journey. I prayed to the Blessed Virgin for guidance. I fretted that a sacred day such as Christmas without a traditional meal from back home would make us ungrateful, forgetting our beginnings, forgetting our true nature. "If we get the banana leaves, maybe, just maybe, everything else will fall into place – Abuela will get the day off, my aunt will feel better, I will make the nacatamales, and we will finally taste America's honey!"

Concentrating on the glorious missionary deeds of Fr. Junipero Serra with the indigenous tribes of California, learning the tiny steps of the new math, and remembering the lessons in St. Paul's letters to the Philippians tested my determination to not listen to the rustling of banana leaves from deep within the borders of Watts. And they rustled every day. This rustling kept piercing my Catholic school good girl resolve, getting louder and louder as each hour of my school day passed. By 2:57 p.m., I had decided to look the devil in his face. I told Mother Superior that Nicholas and I had to help my aunt with her medical appointments, and that we would spend tomorrow's lunch time and after school double cleaning the library. I also told myself that God forgave little white lies during the Christmas season. Watts would be our detour home from school. I never once considered the possibilities that Nicholas often made up stories about his travels here and there or that he often mistook palm trees for banana trees. I wanted to quiz my cousin with flash cards of trees, but decided it was less detrimental to blink into the sun rays than test a nearsighted boy child. We needed banana leaves!

Sometimes the best-laid plans do work out or maybe the stars just properly align. Nicholas' mother had a doctor's appointment and would not be home until late. My younger cousin and I covered our bodies with blessed scapulars purchased on Olivera Street by Abuela (a good report cards treat), kept on our school uniforms (Who would bother innocent-looking Catholic school children?), and made sure our school bags had enough room for our pending horde of fresh banana leaves. The entire round trip excursion to Watts' borderline would take two hours, and there were only two hours and fourteen minutes of daylight left in the sky; being mugged or dying were options not considered part of this journey.

As we were aliens with green cards, the concept of crossing borders came as second nature. We kept a thoroughbred's pace, with our eyes counting the cracks and gum wads on the sidewalks. We smiled at no one. We had no money for sodas or cookies, so we feigned stuffed bellies. With each step, the loudness of the music and scent of the streets grew unfamiliar. This area of Los Angeles displayed ignored grit with a sense of lost opportunity swirling about it. Some big boys breezed by us on bicycles equipped like classic '57 Chevys, but they wanted nothing more than to show off their homemade pride. The more we walked, the less nature followed us, the less daylight signaled a failure. Where were the banana trees? And then Nicholas said he had to pee.

"There's no peeing when you're crossing borders! The Conquistadores did not pee!" I shouted at him. (Back home in Honduras, Nicholas would walk for miles and miles without peeing.

His first visit to a Los Angeles public restroom changed everything. The clean white porcelain bowls and urinals made him a fan of restrooms and erased memories of bushes and weedy growth.)

"I got to go!"

I pointed to a seemingly abandoned lot. "Now make it quick. We don't have much daylight!"

Beyond a junkyard of old cars and even older memories, a loud German Shepherd dog let us know the yard was his. Behind a barrier of dying palm trees, Nicholas relieved himself.

"Hey, why you peeing on my property? This corner belongs to the de Sandoval family!" The voice was not of an angry adult, but a child on guard duty – one probably the same age as Nicholas and just as bewildered.

"Sorry, my cousin had to go! ¡*Lo siento!*" I said when I pulled Nicholas away from dead palms, exhausted cactus, and a broken chain-link fence. There was so much trash, I didn't think Nicholas' wet contribution would be noticed.

"*Lo siento*," Nicholas sheepishly added.

"How come you colored people speak Spanish?"

"We are R&B Spaniards."

"¿*Como?*"

"R&B! Rhythm and blues on the outside and Honduran on the inside," I explained. The junkyard boy did not seem convinced. His eyes dragged across our school uniforms and down to our brogans. We must have looked like true aliens.

"What you guys doing on this side of Avalon Street? Your people live five blocks over by the storefront church."

"— Oh, we have no people — . . ." Nicholas choked in Spanish.

"What he means is that we live by St. Fidelma."

My cousin and I looked at each other, wondering if we should tell the truth. The sky reminded me time was not on the side of liars. "We're looking for banana trees. We need banana leaves for our Christmas dinner."

"Um, you eat bananas leaves? Yuck! We got one in the back yard. I'm Gonzalo de Sandoval. I'm named after an explorer and a co-governor of Mexico. Did you learn about him at your school? What else you eat with them banana leaves? Yuck!"

"And listen," I began, "we don't eat banana leaves – we cook with them. At least we did back home."

Gonzalo de Sandoval stood silent; we stood silent and the sky grew darker.

"Nope. Nope," Nicholas broke the standoff. "Not yet. We're still learning how to be holy and appreciate Abe Lincoln for freeing the slaves," Nicholas explained to Gonzalo de Sandoval.

"We wrap our tamales in the banana leaves. Where are your folks, Gonzalo de Sandoval?" I said, determined to get the leaves and get home. Gonzalo de Sandoval and Nicholas acted like old boys' club friends. No girls allowed. They kick an old beer can as if playing soccer.

"They all went to the hospital to see number seven."

"Number seven?"

"I got another sister!"

"A baby?!"

"Another girl in my life. They all say I am cursed. Our neighbor, Doña Morales, is going to say some special prayers and light seven candles for me."

"Seven is a bad number," I said in Spanish. We all looked at one another, then crossed ourselves. There is nothing worse than a doomed second grader, except maybe a doomed second grader wearing eyeglasses taped at the bridge or one with seven sisters.

"Seven," we moaned in unison. Gonzalo de Sandoval then took Nicholas and me further back into the de Sandoval's compound of odds and ends and discarded dreams. Next to a wooden Craftsman-style house in need of a paint job, a healthy banana tree stood as if in defiance of its tattered surroundings. Some serendipitous moments are best left to speechless awe. Nicholas and I stuffed our school bags with fresh banana leaves after we gave thanks to the Blessed Virgin for our good fortune. Gonzalo de Sandoval knelt with us on his family's lot to give thanks. I took off the scapular blessed by the Holy Father and placed it over Gonzalo de Sandoval's head. I told Nicholas to keep his on because we had an hour of walking with about forty-five minutes of daylight left.

"Yeah, you should run home. Walking takes too long," Gonzalo de Sandoval's advice. "Did you know the Aztecs ran relay races? My mother's father was a white man who left the Dust Bowl. You know about the Okies?"

"What's an Okie?" I asked, but could not wait around for the explanation.

"How come Sister Anne Patrick does not teach us these American things?" my younger cousin demanded. He did not want to be less knowledgeable than his new pal, Gonzalo de Sandoval. I told Nicholas relishing in anger over this educational shortcoming would have to wait for another day.

* * * *

With our school bags filled, December's pending night air reminded us that we were children far away from home with no bus fare, tired legs, and daylight preparing to sleep.

"Hurry, we must get home before your mother returns from the doctor." I tell Nicholas this, but he did not listen to me. He stopped his rapid walk and pointed to a tall man dressed like Abe Lincoln with a stovetop hat standing in front of the Antioch Church of Christ. The man must have been twelve feet tall! There was a crowd of children surrounding him, all jumping, screaming, and grabbing at his elongated fingers.

"There's probably a circus in town," I told Nicholas. "Keep walking. Look at the sky – its color is almost gone! Only slight shades of gray remain."

"Where are the clowns and the wild animals and the big tent?" Nicholas asked.

"Jesus saves!" shouted the man dressed as Mr. Lincoln. But the man was black and had no features like Mr. Lincoln. "Hey little man, do you know what lessons Paul wrote about to the Philippians?" I wondered why Mr. Lincoln, standing in the doorway of a store-front church buffered by a second-hand store and a "you-buy-we-fry" fish eatery, wanted to know about a saint.

My cousin stopped his immediate journey and explained, in perfect English, that St. Paul wrote about fellowship between people on earth. The tall black man smiled, bent down, and gave him a twenty-dollar bill. "Get home now child, get home!" The black Mr. Lincoln smiled and winked at both Nicholas and me.

I grabbed the money from Nicholas' hand and pushed him away from the mob of children salivating over this new wealth. We ran down the street, crossed the railroad tracks at Alameda, and headed toward home, but we were not alone. Four older boys were determined to relieve us of the money. We ran. They ran. They grabbed our book bags. Banana leaves scattered in all directions like dominos, causing one boy to stumble over another. (Saint Fidelma must have been assisting our folly). I prayed a *Hail Mary* very loud – loud enough for an adult to join in. But no one heard my plea. Nicholas joined in, and then a mechanic in coveralls with grease spots and holding a large wrench, moaned out loud a Negro spiritual about freedom and a wild river. Soon, he was joined by a trio harmonizing one of Detroit's latest hits, and the older boys, realizing they were outnumbered, stopped chasing us. And my heart reminded me that I was a child in a country unaware of my Yuletide desires. We continued to push toward home, this time whispering prayers of contrition and watching as streetlights began to turn on block by block, and our prayers lingered above our heads until we shut the front door at 3004 Gramercy Court.

By the time my aunt arrived back home from the doctor, the banana leaf miracle had been seventy-five minutes old. Nicholas and I had eaten our dinner of red beans and corn tortillas, completed our homework, and were thankful our prayers for a good Christmas had been answered: one large banana leaf and the twenty dollar bill lay on the kitchen table. My aunt never asked Nicholas or me for clarifications about the giant Mr. Lincoln or Gonzalo de Sandoval; sometimes it's best not to question miracles lest you upset the angels. On Christmas Eve, Abuela came home, and the sweet potato pie, made by Sister Thelma Johnson, was delivered, but she had forgotten to add the nutmeg and vanilla. She apologized for the pie tasting like "some store-bought pumpkin pie." The collard greens with pork fat were given to another family also in need of food. Oh, and the string to make the doll talk was missing; the doll never spoke a word of hope or about a poor girl missing familiar comforts of back home – poinsettias. But Nicholas's dump truck worked.

The tamales, however, were delicious. Just delicious!

LAUNDRY DAY

(Día de Lavandería)

"To be stupid, selfish, and have good health are
three requirements for happiness, though if
stupidity is lacking, all is lost."

Gustave Flaubert

Whiptail, a town often referred to as its own afterthought, weathered the heat of the desert better than most of its inhabitants. The abrasive realties of the town wore on her face. Someone must have thought it funny to name a town thirty-seven miles dead east of Palm Springs, with no prospect, no coffee shop, no tourist draw, after a lizard whose habitat consisted of sand, barren sand.

She did not find Whiptail funny. The town wore on her mother's face, revealing hues of hard times, disappointing men, and linear battle scars from unsuccessful attempts at happiness. Men. They pictured themselves as captors of Rommel, but without wheels or the authorization to change the drift of the sands.

"That was the past," Magdalena Garcia shouted into the darkness, distracted by an overwhelming heat rush and the sweat that covered her large breasts. She knew she was *pasada*, beyond what eligible men found amusing or tantalizing or easy. *"I'm still a child of God!"*

"Tango." The once hushed word messed around with her emotions as she plucked several long strands of graying hair from her temples. Life did not promise her anything. And she barely remembered what is was like to dance. *"Tango."* She considered herself no better off than the desert rats her cat, Missy Foo, occasionally snuck through the front door; unlike a desert rat, Magdalena kept her tail out of the reach of wild cats. *"Tango."*

Magdalena was stuck. The thrill of boarding an empty box car at the edge of town waned. She dragged on a low-tar cigarette, her cleavage sagging lower with each day, and menopause (according to her gynecologist) was around the corner and impatiently waiting. It was a job – it didn't pay much, but her tips were not shared. *"Tango – turn, then back, two. . . ,"* this time the words brought back the emptiness and pain. With no one to encourage her promenading except an open jar of cold cream and a statue of *La Virgen de Guadalupe*, Magdalena tightened the ankle straps of her dance shoes.

She practiced the graceful moves once taught by her mother. *"Uno, dos, slow steps, then two quick steps, arch . . . Hurry before he gets home, Lena. You must learn to tango."*

"Mama, you can barely see out of that eye."

"Hush, mi hija. Dancing puts the pain on hold. ¡Baile!"

"Pero, Mommie."

"Shhh, no es importante, hija. No es importante."

Remaining in Whiptail was Magdalena's best afterthought. Or at least, the most reasonable. Her life in the town followed a routine with a minimum amount of confusion and worthless men with sweaty palms. And it was the same ten men – three of whom always forgot to dust off the fine grains of desert sand from their boots before they found their way into the hall (a holdover from the town's hey days of railroads) – VFW Post 7551. She removed the dancing shoes tossed them far enough into the closet to forget.

As Whiptail's only source of gossip, regret, and tempered lust, the Veterans of Foreign War Post 7551 occupied the only corner in town with a traffic signal. From eleven in the morning to an hour past sunset, Magdalena served cold beers to white men living with memories of exploding mortars, fallen comrades, and foreign women grateful for liberation by the young, brave, American heroes. Post 7551's current President no longer remembered his own past. The post seemed forgotten, but held on because the old men had nowhere else to hide.

* * * *

A marriage of respect and convenience was what the old vets of Post 7551 sought: they desired younger women to bring them tall glasses of ice water, wipe away high noon sweat from their unkempt brows or help the vets trace the path of their Purple Heart or Medal of Honor. That pathway was clouded with apologies and too much booze and too little tolerance for a nation still not at ease with the end results of wars. A matchmaker would have no problems securing clients, but closing the deal could take some time. However, that was a fine enough arrangement for women who stayed in Whiptail past their prime.

"You must be one of those foreign colored girls, like err, um those major league ball players – err, Cuba? huh?"

"Not me. My parents were refugees from a banana republic on the skids. I came along after they set foot on U.S. soil. I'm as American as cherry pie." (*She didn't tell the Sgt. Major about her mother and her eating cherry pie in the summer – far away from home.)*

"You smell like sweet coconut milk. Hey, you know how to make them tamales?"

"Uh ha." (*She didn't tell the Sgt. Major about her mother and her hiding, waiting until Papi passed out.)*

Magdalena and *el viejo,* Sgt. Major Marion Hopkins, Jr., Retired Army, had both outgrown roadside motels and reneged on promises made to God; she hated the idea of cooking tortillas on a hot plate and he missed a warm body in bed. It was truly a respectable compromise. And his trailer was large enough to escape each other's self-pity.

'I know you don't love me, but if you could find your "America" in comforting an old man's... "

"Shh, you just like feeling my dark skin pressed against your leathery wrinkles, no?" (*She didn't tell the Sgt. Major about her father killing her mother because the cherry pie was cold.*)

"That I do ma'am. That I do."

Their relationship was a breached levee – second thoughts rushed. Some said she wanted his pension. Some said she could have made more waiting on the corner of Pecos and Fourth. The good side of living in Whiptail was no one cared. The marriage ceremony was simple, quiet: a few old Army and Marine buddies drank a toast to the bride and groom and ate cherry cream cake. The newlyweds visited the grave of Magdalena's mother before the night turned into a honeymoon. Sex was not anticipated, just an opportunity for voyeurism by daybreak. They both survived years of emotional floods and people who found their biracial union sacrilegious, un-American. Magdalena and the Sgt. Major lived within their means, but above the desires of others.

Sgt. Major Marion Hopkins, Jr. died on September 23rd. He had actually died twice – once on the fields at Guadalcanal, and the second time in a rain-soaked ditch off Highway 40 on the road to Barstow. He left Magdalena a small pension and a trailer with washer and dryer hook-ups, but no washer or dryer. Wednesdays became the day to clean panties and bras and her soul.

Magdalena respected her role as a widow, but was tired of hand washing, line drying and folding Sgt. Major's red cotton pajamas. Even though the man had been interned at the Desert Memorial Cemetery for ten years, she could not let go of the weekly laundry chore; she visited the local laundromat for everything else – jeans, sheets, kitchen towels. Magdalena was tied up in memories – memories of him, her mother and the man she called *papi*. The day was too hot for a return to a childhood with bruises everyone pretended were not there, cotton candy, and late night talk shows.

The glory days of the VFW hall had been reduced to faded recruit posters and glass curios stuffed with medals, certificates of merit, and even a photo of some of Whiptail's vets with Ike. There was one of a man named Palouse shaking hands with Patton. The stucco building began to sulk like the men who once a year displayed their M1 Garand with pride and debated the experiment of an integrated military unit in Korea. The "big war" soldiers, who called Post 7551 their second home, took their blood streaked nightmares and poured them into double shots or embellished them to interested women needing a place to wait until the desert's heat reached its peaks. Ah, but the aging treetop pilots and their colleagues beleaguered by a

Presidential pardon mused about misplaced homecoming parades and their cash crops hidden deep within the San Bernardino Mountains. These men drank cold beers outside, by the back door to Post 7551. It was safer here than tossing back whiskey with old soldiers who had tasted victory.

The idea for a revival of the veteran's hall began with the death of Seamus J. Winn. The retired Marine colonel had succumbed to lung cancer and hot red peppers three years earlier and had left his widow longing for a way to immortalize his military escapades and patriotic virtues. Mrs. Patsy Winn always seemed to be reliving her glory days as a Missouri high school cheerleader or duties as an ombudsman. Patti, that's what she wanted to be called, was an eighty-one-year-old busybody in pigtails sporting a pink walker. Everyone still found the gray pigtails cute, but out of place in a desert town where residents often forgot to comb their hair. The bold patterns of blue varicose veins on Patti's calves were her only accessorizing flaw.

The tango contest was Patti's fundraiser idea as well as a way of honoring the late colonel. Her dead husband was on the road to immortalization. The contest would be held next Friday night, and a prize of $1000.00 would be given to the best couple.

Two. The tango required two – a number of great distrust, or at least delayed dreams. Magdalena needed a dance partner. Magdalena needed a washer and a dryer. The Wednesday afternoons she spent at the *lavanderia* were becoming a novella starring pregnant immigrants and three drag queens dressed down to keep themselves cool while laundering pink chiffons, orange polyesters, and faux leather.

The tango was in her blood, she thought. It would come back to her just like the visions of her papi hitting her mommie. Everything would work out. She would find a suitable veteran, someone in a uniform fragranced by mothballs and festooned with medals from the battleship *USS California,* now scrapped like the veterans in Whiptail. Magdalena figured any hope for visiting an appliance store in Palm Springs rested with one of those old veterans from Post 7551.

"Ahora si," she thought to herself. *"Yes, now was the opportunity to no longer be a desert exile knee deep in sweaty jeans and coin-dispensed bleach."* Without thinking, she clutched her chest and tangoed right there in the Mother's Helper Laundromat – no music, only flip-flops on her feet. Music filled Magdalena's soul. Soon one of the three drag queens washing her unmentionables joined Magdalena.

"Were you ever in the military?" Magdalena asked.

"No, but I was in several soldiers," Donisha replied with a straight face. This brought chuckles from her two friends watching the impromptu floor show.

"You're going to enter that dance contest, huh, honey?" Topaz shouted as dryer #4 rejected her quarters. "Shit, I hates them dryers!"

"I don't know if I could take one of those old G.I.s feeling all over me."

"Oh, you could Billie Mae! As a matter of fact —"

"Now, now girls. Miss Thing is planning to win and never come back to this quarter wash and fold," said Donisha.

"We'll miss you, Miss Thing!" winked Topaz.

Miss Thing. Was that what she was, a thing? Nondescript, like the patchwork of asphalt that constituted the strip mall's parking lot. What the queens did not realize was Magdalena had a plan. And a desperate woman with a plan was like the desert – undefeatable.

"I haven't won yet . . ." Magdalena griped with sly smile.

"She's got moves you'll never learn!" Topaz snarled at Donisha.

"Up yours, soldier boy, Donald!" commanded Donisha.

"You know there is nothing worse than a queer washerwoman," Billie Mae added.

"Yes there is, this frickin' dry heat. It's going to be in the low 100s all week! Some days the weather gets to me," Magdalena stopped to pour ice water on her head.

"Good old dry heat. I got a little black cocktail dress you could wear," offered Bille Mae.

"Thanks, but I need a partner first, preferably one with a medal or two, and not hooked on booze." Magdalena was desperate to sweep away the grains of time that bound her feet, her youthful delusions.

The monsters she confronted long ago rested beneath the desert's floor. She no longer was a hopeful gypsy dancer, but an arthritic wrinkle with death on the horizon. "Tango!" And the drag queens watched as Miss Thing cleared the laundry's linoleum floor.

* * * *

The men crowded as one, each old soldier hanging onto his bits of sanity, boasting of bloody battle efforts. Magdalena offered a free beer to anyone willing to tango with her. After forty-five minutes, she then offered two beers and two homemade meals, which landed her in the arms of Verdin Lee Sherby. A Marine Captain, Verdin Lee survived the Battle of Van Tuong, but couldn't remember how Vietnam became such a mess. They planned to practice at his trailer on Wednesday; the bar opened at two in the afternoon. Magdalena had the time. Verdin Lee said he would forgo the hall's morning bingo too "Tango a bit with you, ma'am?!"

Blowing labored breaths into Magdalena's earlobes, the sixty-eight-year-old was lost somewhere in Argentina, wearing oversized gaucho boots and a heating pad. Arthritis was the reason for his move to the high desert. A widower living in space H-15 at Lizard Creek Motor Park with Gladys, his Tibetan black terrier, and the wooden-framed portraits of his children, grandchildren and one of his dead wife, which he twine-tied to his entry gate. He lamented about his carousing and an understanding wife, and how he never got to explain about those last days in Saigon. That was all in the past; his only concentration was acclimatizing to the hot desert air.

"We always seem to be out of time, but not to know it."

"I'm pretty liberal for an old fart from Olive Hill, Kentucky, you know. I fought alongside your people in Nam," Verdin Lee proclaimed.

"Really? There were Hondurans in Vietnam?"

"Hon ... Hon, what?"

"So, where did you learn to tango?"

"My wife, God rest her soul, thought I should learn the classical dances. You know, I supported Truman's Executive Order 9981." Verdin Lee's wiry fingers moved over Magdalena's shoulders as he tried to make conversation.

"Nice photos. Your family?"

"Yeah! Worthless. All of them."

"Your children love you, no?"

"My son calls once a month, and my daughter remembers me only at Christmas."

"What kind of father were you, Verdin Lee?"

"The kind that served this country well, but drank too much."

"And you used your fists too much?"

Verdin Lee gave a slight grin and pressed his cheek against hers. They spoke no more about family, only about the mutual acquaintances they had made in Whiptail. The conversations were brief, dangling in the still air like pussy willows. Verdin Lee moved closer to Magdalena, hoping to practice longer than the thirty minutes the two beers had bought. He told her he just wanted to dance. Magdalena hesitated, smiled, and lit a cigarette as the practice continued. Her hands would be spared the cheap bleach Verdin Lee kept on his kitchen counter. Within the ninety minutes their bodies bumped and missed the mark, he whispered, "excuse my big feet" six times, and she realized that teaching an old vet to tango was much like Verdin Lee's dead wife – a chance for forgiveness lost.

"You know, Magdalena, the tango is not a dance for lovers. It is a dance for restless souls."

"It's four o'clock. We have no music. Maybe you would like to take a break." (She didn't tell Verdin Lee her mother said the same thing the day she died.)

"Nah, I got all the time in the world," Verdin Lee just held on even tighter. Had he heard her, or maybe he hadn't? It was a chance she took. Free was not worth yelling about, and anyway, being ignored had its benefits. Magdalena released a puff of smoke which made Verdin Lee's eyes glisten with youthful joy. He moved closer to her, his emphysematous reaching a raspy crescendo. They danced for one more hour.

"Pretty good for an old guy without music, huh?"

"Yes, your wife taught you well."

"We would tango on Saturday afternoon when the kids preferred the company of their friends. We sometimes danced beyond supper time. The kids would yell for something to eat, and we'd end up at some burger joint." Verdin Lee laughed at this glimpse into his past.

"Muy bueno, pretty good." Magdalena forced a dry smile. Maybe that new washer and dryer would be hers yet. Teacher and student rested in lawn chairs twenty years beyond their summertime prime. Magdalena rubbed her ankles, and Verdin Lee tossed back a warm whiskey shot.

"I always thought you and Marion made a great twosome," Verdin Lee said. His small talk became the rhythm to which Magdalena dreamed. She heard nothing and thought about how she'd miss the antics of the women and would-be women at the lavanderia. She took a long draw from a cigarette, holding the smoke longer than she wanted. The cotton dress, now wet, caressed what feminine outline she had left. She caught Verdin Lee giving her a carnal once-over.

"You like dancing, Verdin Lee?" she asked as smoke covered the mess in the old vet's yard.

"I think you're still pretty hot stuff," Verdin Lee moved closer to Magdalena, even as she pumped smoke in his direction. "I hope you realize that life is nothing but a series of last-minute compromises."

"Last minute," Magdalena repeated softly to herself. "Yes, I guess you're right, Verdin Lee. Shall we begin again?" The old man closed his eyes, becoming lost in a passion long forgotten. Magdalena thought about her mother and wondered if the Blessed Mother was still keeping her safe.

The day waned with orange skies and wispy clouds. The desert prepared for its silent, cool dawn. Exhausted with pleasure, Magdalena walked pass the VFW. The circumstance of the contest would be left until tomorrow night's breezes. And the desert was always unpredictable about its sudden gusty winds.

Verdin Lee's arthritic hands dusted the sand from his best dress marching boots. Magdalena had never seen that many honor bars. He tried to remember why he was awarded so many, thirty-eight in all. She placed his arms around her girdle-cinched waist. The old vet had come to her rescue. The musicians prepped their fingers with bourbon shots. *"Adiós muchachos, compañeros de mi vida... "* The Carlos Gardel tune resonated in Magdalena's nostalgia. Verdin Lee had never heard it played until that night. It was the musicians' attempt to remind the contest participants and audience that this was a serious venture. More booze and the contest was underway. Verdin Lee cuddled his partner with a grace only the saints in heaven could have mustered up. Reassured, Magdalena lost herself in the music of her mother's pain. She tossed her head from the left, then from the right. Her legs and his legs were eking out slow sensual steps. This was right, she just knew it. And just like a clumsy twelve-year-old dancer learning to tango on her mother's freshly mopped linoleum floor, Magdalena remembered the steps: 1, 2, 3, 4. Turn halfway. 1, 2, 3, 4. The tango was back in her soul. And so was the time when she stepped on her mama's toes; and the time she turned into the cutting board, sending onions and red peppers everywhere; and the time she fell onto the kitchen floor giddy with laughter and a little regret. Magdalena thought about the strange mixture of patrons at the lavandería. Wednesday seemed so far off.

COWHAND

"There will come a time when you believe everything
is finished. That will be the beginning."

Louis L'Amour

Before I knew the words *city slicker, plum loco, sidewinder,* I learned the word *stepfather*. There were days when that word caused me to gag like the calf's liver Abuela forced me eat. In letters Mama sent back home, she wrote of an hombre from Texas who rode horses and changed her world. The handwritten apologies described a man over six feet who owned property and was a wounded war veteran. Abuela and I were puzzled. We expected the letters to tell us when Mama would send for me or at least send money for sacks of rice and red beans and my upbringing. I pictured her and him galloping into sunsets as all cowboys did. Truth be told, the tall Texan mainly placed bets on thoroughbreds. And my mother fell into his myth of true love.

Mama married the Texan and wanted me to join their blissful living arrangement; however, the money was too tight and the legal passage was too expensive and the Texan was not sure I would adjust to the Lone Star State. I was to be patient. I would be in America soon enough. In preparation for my journey, *Abuela* took me to see Hollywood Westerns which played every Friday at the theater in our village of Paseo Santa Rosa. I watched Roy Rogers sing about being a cowhand from the Rio Grande. *YIPPIE YI YO KAYAH!* I gasped as John Wayne punched out a wicked man, and watched Dale Evans sing to the man she loved in a low-cut evening gown. I pictured mother singing, in a gathered *falda* with red and yellow rick-rack, *Corrido de Honduras* to the Texan.

Armed with confidence that I would be living in Texas, I practiced what English words I knew with a slight Texan drawl. I felt prepared to live in America. I watched those Western movies so many times I knew the pitfalls of the Code of the West. I had my Abuela read Zane Grey and Louis L'Amour stories to me and memorized the facial contours of real cowboys. I reconciled my skill to walk bow-legged with the nickname "cowhand," as Abuela began to call me. For months upon months, the church women's seetful talk about how my mama probably forgot about her *only* child as she made a new family, one without the entanglements of an older child, chafed the tender spots on my body worse than my rawhide chaps. If I were Annie Oakley, why I would . . . Yup! Yup! Ending up an old woman in a white church dress who sat with her legs spread as if awaiting a basket of red beans that needed to be sorted before cooking was not in the cards for me. Yup! I found the idea of singing to horses an easier trail to follow than being knee deep in diapers, tortillas, and unfulfilled dreams. I wanted to become the next Dale Evans – a colored Dale Evans.

* * * *

Yes, I sure surmised things would not be as easy as I had imagined. Abuela's tears and anger in her heart for my mother became a two-step dance: we prayed to *la Virgen de Guadalupe* at each of the three altars Abuela had in her small house. We ate refried red beans with handmade tortillas and pumped the organ for the Mormons' sacrament meetings. Abuela's musical gift paid for me to see Texas.

The details of border crossings are never made clear. Besides, without *proper papers,* as everyone in Paseo Santa Rosa knew, journeying to America was a shadowy endeavor. Abuela took no chance with the money she made playing the organ for the missionaries. She had Naluma bless a handkerchief with special herbs; then Abuela wrapped spending money in it and pinned it inside my sox.

"¡Vamos!" A man in a NY baseball cap packed us into a truck blueprinted for fewer passengers.

It was my last day as a grandchild. A new beginning had been promised in Abuela's last sermon to me. With tears falling over her cheeks, it didn't matter those nosy old church women were within listening distance – *another time we will meet in the eternal paradise.*

* * * *

At the age of nine, I waded across the Rio Grande on the shoulders of a man whose name people only whispered pass sunset – C*oyote.* I crossed the Sonora Desert into the real America in the back of a white pickup camper. As the gloaming desert hues grappled with my young conscience, I crouched as low as I could in the old pickup desperate to see the western sky of *los Estados Unidos.* The desert's costumes of tumbleweed, sagebrush, and loose gravel befitted the unshaven Coyote and his cargo of two Honduran children, three Mexican women, one Guatemalan woman, and one old man not wishing to die until he met his grandchildren. We were crammed into a space allotted for four, and the space had obviously been used to carry bushels of onions in various degrees of decay.

Where were the pastel painted skies and majestic rock formations? The white pickup, which revealed more and more evidence of crimes, passed the border patrol officers with a gentleman's grin and nod. My belly ached, and the skirt Grandmother had made smelled of stale urine which had escaped my will and the wills of others. I overheard the three women moan about being dumped in the middle of nowhere or worse, being something they only mouthed to each other. I yearned for Abuela's jokes, her handmade tamales, and the comfort of her arms. What would the women from Saint Leo's say about me now? I was dirty, and being colored and dirty was never a good poker hand in America.

The drive across the dry riverbed was a wild bronco ride; we bounced left to right and up and down in the old truck. I kept count of how many times my head bucked into the knees of the other passengers in order to keep awake. *Abuela* had said I was to trust no one. The aloneness of the journey gave me the opportunity to converse with Jesus. I asked Him why there were no colored cowboys in Hollywood. I imagined stallions and palominos trotted the streets of Los Angeles like true movie stars.

Eventually, the white pickup truck parked beside a liquor store selling cold drinks. The Coyote shouted, "Mojave!" He pulled each one of us from the pickup, including the grandfather, then drove off. "Your families will get you from here!" he yelled in Spanish back to us as an afterthought. Maybe the Texan would show up ridding a winning horse.

"¡Basta!" "¡Basta!" the women shouted, waving their fists and calling the Coyote's mother *unwashed*. We all were unwashed.

I had figured Los Angeles as having tall buildings and a movie studio on each corner. There was nothing in this place except for the liquor store with cold drinks; they also sold handheld fruit pies – peach, apple, and something called olallieberry. The pies and other foods were dry, tired, and picked over. We folded our arms as if mourners saying *adiós* for the last time. No one offered to help. The few white people touring the Mojave said they would call immigration on our group of smelly, Spanish-speaking intruders. I felt abandoned like the American Indian, but I was featherless and had no face paint to wage war. "Those darn pale faces!" I mumbled.

Not one cowboy came riding high in his saddle with a twinkle in his blue eyes to rescue me. The old grandfather said that I would not feel the water as yet, but that my back was wet, and people with wet backs were not supposed to be in America. He told me wetbacks kept quiet, moved invisibly, and asked the Blessed Mother to end their fears. "¡*Miedo*! ¡*Miedo*!" He lamented as his sunburned head bowed in deference to the Blessed Mother. But I was the next Dale Evans – I feared no one.

It took another day and a night of counting stars for all of us to be reunited with our people. Mojave was a desert much farther from Los Angeles than I had expected, but Los Angeles was a place to start all over – again.

* * * *

Mama's new husband was no cowboy. Thomas Charles Jackson, a tall black man, did not even own a cowboy hat and demanded hot water cornbread on Sunday mornings. I figured this hot water mush was a habit for all Southerners. Mama only knew how to make corn tortillas. Mr. Jackson was a veteran with a piece of Nazi shrapnel still embedded in his head. The American government had helped him buy an old motel and a used car. I think they were tired of listening to Mr. Jackson's stories of World War II and the bullet that almost ended his life. Mr. Jackson owned no horses, but liked to see the "ponies run." And because of this, Mama had to make beds in the motel even though she was pregnant. She never sent for Abuela, and Abuela stopped playing the organ for the missionaries a month before she died. I became a cowhand – I fixed things: tightened screws, unclogged toilets, but never rode into the sunset like Dale Evans. I helped Mama clean the motel rooms, learned to make hot water cornbread, and minded my new half-sister when mama and Mr. Jackson went to see his ponies run. And for services rendered, he made a name tag for me; it read, D-A-L-E.

Unlike Dale Evans, I had no backlot trailer or white fringed, western style cowgirl shirt to wear while rehearsing my lines to fool *la migra.* With tacit reckoning, Mr. Jackson saw to it that I became a black and proud schoolgirl listening to soul music and missing my southern fried, magnolia hometown roots.

My border had expanded from Abuela's dirt yard with chickens too fastidious to be a Sunday dinner to California, where "Hollywood" was just a sign on a hill three bus rides away from the smaller perimeters of South-Central L.A.; where my tongue was untied, and the dreams of the West disappeared like the Tongva people who once owned Los Angeles. For the descendants of the Tongva tribe, the L.A. Basin was a "once upon a time" place and Abuela and back home were just as fleeting for me. The scapular of *la Virgen* worn around my neck was replaced with one with the gold and red colors of St. Eligius – the saint protecting horses, and on good days, guaranteeing an exacta win.

The seasons for thoroughbreds arrived, and Mr. Jackson placed me on a carousel horse during a weekend when a government-sponsored carnival passed through South-Central L.A.

"Ride it!" My stepfather shouted at me. "He's a real bronco! Yahoooo!" The horse was blacker than black, with a painted-on golden saddle, and grinned as if it knew all my venial sins. That *caballo* whispered with a grin that I was now home, never to see Honduras again, and night tears would change nothing. Mr. Jackson died six hours later. The carnival and its crew were headed for the San Fernando Valley before his body was buried. Mr. Jackson's veteran friends said he finally ate the bullet. I said twenty Hail Marys that night, then told myself the late Mr. Jackson was just that – *late*.

Mama said that Mr. Jackson had a ticket for a black horse that paid 30:1. Our backs are now dry, and Mama, Anna (my half-sister), and I never worried about cleaning the hotel rooms ever again. The Mojave Desert still maintains its ability to create mirages, allowing the duped tenderfoot to be lassoed into silence. You know, silence is a forgiving bedfellow, understanding tales from the border. As a good Catholic school girl, I prayed for my stepfather's dead soul every night until I was eighteen years old. He was then placed in our family's pantheon of misunderstood souls. I do have days when I remember the smell of urine on rotten onions skins. On those days, I take a drive to where the solitude of the Mojave welcomes smugglers and dreamers, and I visit a liquor store to see if its supply of Dale's Fruit Pies needs replenishing. *They're the best in the West! YIPPIE YI YO KAYAH!*

SPRING IN THE SCREECH OWL'S BARN

"Things are always better in the morning."

Harper Lee

The owl's nestbox hid trinkets: rabbit bones, a sapphire button, restless words. The owl could not recall a time when the ghosts were more benevolent. The old barn had been settling among the wild mustard fields just west of El Camino Real – silent while its bright red cloak faded to a rusty red, a dull semblance of what had been. The barn had been abused by nature's timing, and now another spring meant the return of old memories. Inside the barn, a screech owl worked the aril of a snatched almond and exacerbated the mild discontent of the barn's landlady. The son had been drinking, and the mother paused to listen to the rapid verbiage of his daytime hallucinations. The barn obliged as it always had, fine tuning the volume of regret.

As with all good war-worn commanders, the mother braced for the deluge of accusations. She and he were blood relatives, not friends; they were a keeper and a kept. The scrimmages were a reoccurring cadence of misjudgments on her part and a drug-induced rouse on his.

Misjudgments. Yes, she did not understand his flight pattern – it was easier to stare into the black sky. This was the closest they would come to forgiveness. They both had abandoned their comfortable fantasies. How did a vintage bamboo birdcage from India warrant such deviant discourse?

A half smile tickled the mother's upper lip; she remembered an insistent *niño* – a male child who only wanted attention. And she willingly gave it without hesitation. *Mom! Mom! Can we keep Mr. Kelly over the weekend? He's the class pet rat. Please! Please!*

It was just a birdcage. A birdcage. An empty house for a winged creature never purchased, never realized. *Melocanna, melocanna – bamboo, Mom!* The mother nodded to herself. Was that third or fourth grade?

"It's not big enough for the screech owl," the besotted son confided to his true pal – a pint of the corner store's cheapest gin.

"Screech owl?" The mother thought she had missed something.

"Yeah, the screech owl. Cage it up!"

The mother responded with the calm she kept just behind her heart, "Screech owls are free; they require only rodents and other small finds to ward off hunger pangs and dilapidated barns in which to hide." *Please Mom! Pleaseeee.* "I mean . . . owls don't belong in cages, Benito." Her words easily leaped from her mouth, becoming a part of the constellation of excuses that have always hung from the rafters in the old barn. "Owls need space to explore, not a cage."

"You'll probably ruin that, too. It would had been better if you were my teacher instead of my mother." The mother listened to her son, nodded and thought to herself that it would have been better to have known the name of her son's street pharmacist.

"Could you put down that bot —" the mother began.

"No Mom! You can't tell me what to do. I should have . . ." The son's sentence blended into the silence of the barn's worn wood. He inhaled the crispness of the spring air, puffed out his chest like a warbler, and stood inches from his mother's face, holding the gin bottle to his lips, then tossing it aside.

Mom, can I have another chocolate chip cookie? It will make the bedtime story so much better, pleaseeee.

"Where's the photo? The silver frame is missing its photo," the mother added to the scrimmage, changing the subject, changing the focus of their challenge, their lack of harmony.

"What photo? I don't know what you're talking about, Mom."

"It was the only one I had of our . . ."

"Ah, ah you, you mean 'happy family?' You're a whore, Mom. A whore. I'm sorry for saying that, but you are one. You like only the finer things in life, and I am not fine at all."

The mother looked at her son, seeing the child she had wanted more than life, and the toxicity he had become to himself and to her. Their conversation now somersaulted deep within her stomach, making her sick to think this is what had become of a dream. She laughed, "Yes, I guess I am a whore. Whores suffer with a smile on their faces, cry in their sleep, and live without love for long periods of time." *What color is the sky? Where do moths come from, Mom? Can I spend the night at Taylor's? Why can't we keep the baby owl in that old cage, huh, huh?*

"Mom?" The son shouted.

"I've been wrapped up in a hurricane wind since you've been back. I love you, but you need hel—"

"I need only myself, Mom. And the cage? You never used it. You never wanted it!"

"I'm afraid you'll end up like a lost soldier or like that rap singer or like people your age who have no real direction." The words never meant for his ears stepped over everything. Now she feared the worst.

"You'd like that, huh? You'd be free, Mom. F-R-E-E!"

The mother closed her eyes. That was the freedom she had needed, the freedom they both had deserved, like a good night's sleep. The mother shoved the bamboo cage onto the floor and watched as its small door became crushed under the cage's weight. The mother had one succinct thought as she eyeballed the son's spirit leaving the barn – no confrontation today she said to herself. No meth or cheap gin. No confrontation today!

The screech owl had lingered much too long over the performance in the barn – too much resentment, resignation, hesitation. It was the favorable mention of love that had caused the owl to remain flightless. The mother left the barn, her steps less painful than when she had entered. The owl wondered which Spring would bring the acknowledgment of the son's death. And on what day in Spring she would sell the broken bamboo cage. There was no confrontation today. It was near dusk – the anniversary will begin at dawn. The barn exhaled, eked out a slight moan – tomorrow would take care of itself.

LA LUZ DEL MUNDO

(Light of the World)

" . . . children are a heritage from the Lord,

the fruit of the womb, a reward."

Psalm 127:3

At 1:37 this afternoon, I became a citizen. The worst part about reaching this pinnacle was the years spent bent over cleaning toilets and making beds which were usually last occupied by men entertaining their miseries; sometimes these miseries were two hundred dollars a night, sometimes they were dragged from cars with black windows.

My own grace was too illegal to help those girls. I prayed for their bodies and souls. They have never left my thoughts. Raul, my grandson, asks questions about my long journey here and why at night

I light a candle and leave it in the front window. I say it is a guiding beacon. He looks at me because he does not understand the word *beacon*. I tell him about the ghost and how the inner light the ghost possessed shined on my dirty face and saved me. "Ah, Abuelita," he giggles, "you are old Mexico. No one believes in ghosts." He then runs off to play with other children like himself, unaware of the grace bestowed on their families: never hungry, never afraid, never alone. In those days, we were the unwashed aliens and always, always hungry: hungry for jobs, hungry for life – not table scraps. When you plot to do wrong in the name of hunger, you become selfish – you want no one else to be fed. Yet, all mouths are open wide. It was the ghost who closed my mouth and took control of my fears. I realized Americans were hungry too, but their hunger was satisfied with peanut butter and jelly.

There were fifteen of us, each resisting and deflecting the urge to run back home instead of forward, following strange men through an unknown desert. To keep the younger children quiet, moving, and less curious, the older girls like myself were told to divert their hunger pangs and fright: we circulated lies made into truths – *American farmers need us. The pizzas are the size of a wooden cartwheel.*

As we got closer to the town of Jacumbra, many of the younger girls disappeared. Gone – leaving no memory of their dreams! I felt about in the darkness, dreading scorpions, but finding only their empty water containers. My own body ached, my heart suspended its beating, my soul grappled with the idea of living in a place imprinted onto my life by technicolor movies and cousins working in America. I tell you, I was full of fear. Then a girl, not much older than myself, untwisted the dreams from my stomach and illuminated them, giving them importance. She lay next to me, and I learned how the blindness in which she crossed the desert was molded from a dream that bound her chest and decayed her soul. She told me she would be my light, and when the men came, she and I hovered above them, singing songs from our childhood; they could never really hurt us. The girl dried my tears with stories of her transformation from girl to boy, from wetback to ghost, before the men with wretched male urgencies ordered me to move. I was no longer afraid of the darkness. She told me she was *La Luz del Mundo,* but her mother, Maria Pinkus, had called her Consuelo. She told me it was the *brujas*, three of them, who laid their shriveled hands on her head the day she was born, and it was the same three old women who told her mother her youngest girl child would be the light for those in fear. Her mother thought she was raising a saint, not a dark soul beacon.

* * * *

Consuelo Maria Pinkus was too white to be Mexican, and the road she lived on was too uneven to be prosperous. Her sunrise prayers to the Catholic saints were too full of hope to be taken seriously; even Jesus sighed. Consuelo's desire was to be *La Luz del Mundo,* even though she pictured herself dull – no shining beacon. She wanted to rescue people just the way the Virgin Mary had saved people in distress, in need.

Consuelo's light began as a faint glow. One day she was told to gather several yellow flowers from an agave plant for the anniversary of her grandmother's death. The grave had to be cleaned and decorated as families in her village did for their dead once a year. "The agave is a beautiful plant with pretty little flowers and succulent leaves until your skin is pricked by its needles," her mother cautioned. Consuelo did not hear her mother's warning; she was too busy following the path of a lizard which crawled under their dwelling. She nodded her head and ran down the road to where a clump of agave grew. Her mother shouted something about praying to the Aztec goddess *Mayahuel* for protection from the needles, but Consuelo's hands had already felt the prick of the agave among the patchwork of bright yellow flowers. Her steps back home were slower than her steps to the agave clumps, and her hands and some of the flowers were stained with blood. Consuelo remembered the joy of her Abuelita, but forgot to pray to the goddess.

The yellow flowers were set aside as Consuelo's mother used cool water to rinse off the blood from Consuelo's hand. "You are the sweetness of the earth, my daughter," her mother said. The words did not hold true, for the mud Consuelo was eating at the time tasted bitter and scratched her throat as she swallowed it. Sweet lies. You see, we women have a limitless supply of sweet lies. They are repeated by mothers to daughters on hot summer afternoons when there was nothing left to eat and the *agua fresca* made with old mangoes had become hot and watery.

"I'll love you until your pigtails plait themselves." The mother's words then landed on the floor just like the strands of hair clutched in her hands before shiny black scissors bobbed Consuelo's hair. And in the mirror, a new silhouette stood dressed in lace to honor the Blessed Virgin, but looking more like a Carlos than a Consuelo. Maria Pinkus had four girls; one had made the crossing then died pursuing a white man who thought all Mexican women were Conchitas-on-the-make, and the oldest – twins – stayed by their mother's side, afraid of all men except Jesus. That was the first day Consuelo understood the secret of being a woman.

"I blame Maximilian's men and your great-grandmother Dolores for your fair skin and blue eyes. If you were dark like your sisters or the Maya, or short and fat like them too, your life would be a daily routine of labor and suffering – nothing special. I would have many grandchildren and spend my days dwindling into death fussed over by you and them," Consuelo's mother grumbled. "One day, you will appreciate this change, my daughter." Maria Pinkus gave her youngest child strips of cloth torn from an old white sheet to bind her tender breasts, which were developing. "I do all this work for you, *mija.* No one can say that I am not a good mother."

"You're a saintly mother," Consuelo comforted.

"No saint, just a sinner with ample years of suffering to warrant some grace."

Consuelo's mother then said boys strayed far from their mothers in pursuit of better endings. They listened instead to the wind, argued with themselves, and fought each other over women. Boys have only strength to offer, not feelings from their hearts.

For Consuelo, the change from girl to boy was gradual. Her lightheartedness disappeared in bits, day by day. It took practice to speak with a boy's determination and keep her head and fists held up. Her new shape allowed the arrogance to roughhouse with Miguel and Pepe, hit home runs, and indulge in sips of warm beer offered by the old men at the *zocalo* as they boasted and reminisced about their own virile accomplishments. Their stories, as old as the men themselves, lived on toy train tracks which choo-chooed in circles again and again and again.

People of Consuelo's village believed the labyrinth of immigration was a tricky game. It assumed the participant was plenty hungry, not a bamboozled victim. Consuelo missed wearing colorful ribbons in her hair and paid an extremely high price for crossing the desert into *el norte.* The snakes were more cunning than the one that plagued Eve, and the two-legged Coyotes were more dangerous than the four-legged ones. Those men calculated the width of a young boy's hips and spread Consuelo's legs even wider. It was the light that saved the silhouette. The light from the café's sign across the paved road where Americans drank black coffee and ate hamburgers: EAT AT JOE'S! COLD BEER INSIDE! The lights were new; they made the ugly seem pretty and they disguised the bitterness of the asphalt road.

Adolescent girls pretending to be adolescent boys are malleable, with a dogged sense of survival. The Coyotes used the backs of their hands to wipe away the saliva after their reckless fun. They laughed as if beer drunk. Each congratulated the other, and each counted the hundred dollar bills *el viaje* pocketed. By the time Consuelo was stripped of her earthly frame, her silhouette had moved with an archangel's pliancy and had settled behind the neon letter "C" of the café sign. There was no one to fuss over her in the daylight. The sun was too glaring for Consuelo to see beyond the rising heat of the desert's floor. The sun was too powerful to see her own splayed body or watch mother coyotes feed their babies with her flesh. You see, at night Consuelo became one with the neon lights. She watched as tourists, old drunks and lost young girls used the café as the crossroads in their journey. Consuelo became the light in the desert for girls pretending to not be themselves. She would rescue one, and one would rescue another, and in return, Consuelo's ghost would live forever behind the letter C where the Coyotes could never find her. Never get her.

Many nights in those early years, I searched for Consuelo, but found only girls – girls like I once was – in need of the light. I showed them the neon sign – EAT AT JOE'S! COLD BEER INSIDE! And then I told them they were in the grace of a ghost, and their souls were now free to dream.

ACKNOWLEDGMENTS

I wish to thank Miranda, Peggy, Diana, Stella, Billie, and the women at *Patch* for pushing me and these stories to this point. I could not have done it without all of you. You read, cried, commented, argued over this manuscript.

For his unconditional love and patience and many years of saying, "Yes, you can write," my husband Rich.

¿Pues, Grandmamá, qué piensa usted?

Made in the USA
San Bernardino, CA
23 February 2020